For Rebecca Gray Wells
—T.T.

To my granddaughter "Spunken" Victoria
—H.S.

Wishes for You • Text copyright © 2003 by Tobi Tobias • Illustrations copyright © 2003 by Henri Sorensen • Manufactured in China. All rights reserved. • www.harperchildrens.com • Library of Congress Cataloging-in-Publication Data • Tobias, Tobi • Wishes for you / by Tobi Tobias ; illustrated by Henri Sorensen. • p. cm. • Summary: A series of wishes for a child's bright and hopeful future. • ISBN 0-688-10838-5—ISBN 0-688-10839-3 (lib. bdg.) • [1. Wishes—Fiction. 2. Family—Fiction.] I. Sorensen, Henri, ill. II. Title. • PZ7.T56 Wi 2003 • [E]—dc21   2001024372 • Typography by Robbin Gourley and Jeanne L. Hogle • 1 2 3 4 5 6 7 8 9 10 • ❖ • First Edition

Wishes for You

BY TOBI TOBIAS

ILLUSTRATED BY HENRI SORENSEN

HarperCollins*Publishers*

I hope you will have moments when you're so happy,
you'll feel the sun is shining from inside you.

I hope you will have the strength and spirit
to deal with bad things
when they come your way.

I hope you will be lucky.

I hope you will always be curious.

I hope you will never forget
how to be silly.

I hope you and I will have adventures together—
just the two of us.

I hope you will love to read.

I hope you will learn how to make things
with your own hands.

I hope you will want to make your body strong
and quick and beautiful—and enjoy the way that feels.

I hope you will love one special person
more than anyone or anything
in the whole world.

I hope that, one day when you're grown up,
you will have a child—different from you,
but just as wonderful.

I hope you will know what you think and feel and not let other people tell you.

I hope you will be able to tell your favorite people the secrets of your heart.

I hope you will always be part of a family.

I hope you will always remember me
and know how much I love you.